THE GODMOTHER

For Judy and Iris, my lovely godmothers

With special thanks to Karin, Guido, Willem, Joost and Pim

THE GODMOTHER

S.R. Harris • Illustrated by Helen van Vliet

S & F

When you are born there's always a Mum.
There might be a Dad. And there could be brothers or sisters if you're lucky
(or unlucky, as my brother likes to point out, when he's fed up with me).
And that's your family, more or less.

But sometimes there is someone else. Like Sam.

I've got this photo of her holding me in the church. I'm a baby and I'm being christened.

I'm wearing this white frilly dress that makes me look like a meringue.

Except for my face. It's so red it's turned into an apple. A cross apple.

Sam is rocking me gently in her arms.

Maybe God put her there to cheer me up?

SHE GAVE ME A CANDLE THAT DAY. It sits on our mantelpiece.

On the side it says, 'Emma, your name is engraved in the palm of God's hand'.

He must have very big hands and they must be full of tattoos.

Dear Emma,
My cat's called Dopey. He sleeps so much.
I wonder what he's dreaming about?
Love from your godmother,
Sam

OUR FRIDGE became covered in postcards from Sam. I called them Samgrams.
Other grown-ups tell you things but she always asked questions.
I stared at the picture of the cat she sent me and wondered
if it dreamt of the mice that got away.

W E SENT A LOT OF SAMGRAMS TO EACH OTHER.

Dear Emma,

I have started painting the windows in my cottage.
There are four at the front and four at the back.
There's a door at the front and one at the back.
Should they be in the same colour?

Love,
Sam

Nobody had ever asked me something like that before.

Dear Sam,
I think they should be in the same colour
because otherwise you will have to by too
sorts of paint.

Love,
Emma

Blue's my faverit colour.

SOMETIMES SHE CAME TO STAY WITH US. She was like a parcel that plopped through the post on a rainy day when I didn't know what to do. She let me unwrap her and there was a surprise to every layer. She knew how to make grass whistle. She taught me to play chess. She could make a hat out of a shopping list.

In her pocket I once found a baby hamster.

We went out together to choose a cage and bought one with a slide and a wheel and a little swing.

We peered at the hamster through the bars and wished we were small enough to join him.

I thought Sam was sure to have a potion for that. Maybe she was a fairy godmother? She fished out some sweets from the bottom of her bag and we tried those.

It didn't work. We were still the same size.

WHEN SHE STAYED WITH US she used to tell me stories in bed in the morning.
She wore woollen socks because her feet got cold and large shirts that smelt of lavender.
She was never in a hurry. She told me about the hospital where she worked, the sheep that lived
on her doorstep, the beaches with grey sand where you find mussels clinging to the rocks,
the tall black mountains called the Cuillins that you can see from her garden.

SHE TOLD ME SHE GOT PHONE CALLS in the middle of the night
because she was a Samaritan.
'What's a Samaritan?' I asked.
'Someone who listens,' she said.
'I like listening to your stories,' I told her.
'I like having someone to tell them to,' she said.

SHE LIKED ME TO TELL HER THINGS TOO. She wanted to know what I liked doing best. I had to think a lot about that. It was probably painting.

'What was my favourite food?' Spaghetti. I knew that.

'My favourite stories?' 101 (and 102) Dalmatians. I've got the video and I've seen the film.

'My favourite day of the week?' Saturday.

'My favourite time of year?' Summer.

I didn't know there was so much to know about me.

She wanted to know what my teacher was like, my school, my best friend even.

I told her my best friend was called Julie.

'Your mum's my best friend,' Sam said.

THAT'S WHEN I FOUND OUT it wasn't God who'd put her there that day in the church when she tried to make me laugh. It was Mum.

'I wanted her to be your godmother,' Mum said. 'Because of the way she looks at life. She sees things differently to other people. She's interested in everything and she's got so much patience.'

She told me they were at school together and Sam was always the naughty one.

'What did she do?' I asked.

'Turned the whole place upside down,' she replied.

I liked the sound of that. I was practising handstands by then against the sitting-room door so I knew what the world looked like when you were standing on your head.

SOMETIMES I WENT TO STAY WITH SAM. She lives in a place called Skye. It's an island in the north-west of Scotland. It's very beautiful with sheep and mountains and mist and lots and lots of sky. She told me it changed colour all the time so she always had something to watch.

I loved going to stay with her. It was as if we were driving to the end of the world. It was all rocks and water and sheep roaming over the road. I was sure if we went any further we would fall off. There weren't any fences any more and the mountains disappeared into clouds. My heart always beat faster and a tingly, tangly feeling jiggled in my stomach like a Highland fling.

When I first went to her house, we could hardly find the front door, the garden was so overgrown. There were sheep grazing everywhere and a cat sunning itself on the roof.

'This is your room,' Sam said, 'whenever you want to come and stay. I've just finished painting it.'

Blue! Just like her doors and windows.

Her kitchen was stacked with cups and plates and saucepans of soup and the phone was always ringing. 'Let's make bread,' she said, pushing everything to one side. 'And we'll eat it when we get hungry.' I thought of our kitchen back home with everything in its place and three meals a day in the right order. 'Mum would never let us do this,' I told her. 'We always have to lay the table and have lunch at lunch-time and eat everything that's on our plate.'

Sam thought that sounded wonderful. 'We can have special times together, you and me, but your mum's made a home for you, day in, day out. Later on you'll remember how comforting it was when you knew that, whatever happened out there in the world, at one o'clock there would always be lunch and at four o'clock there would always be tea.'

I sighed. That seemed like an awful lot of meals.

SHE WAS OFTEN LOSING THINGS. Her glasses. The letter with the electricity bill
(she didn't mind about that, she said), the top of the lemonade, the keys of the car even.
I always seemed to be able to find them.
'You're so clever,' she told me.
But I didn't know I was good at finding things till she lost them.

'WHEN I'M GROWN UP I want to be like you,' I told her.

We were sitting at the kitchen table painting pictures of Dopey.

He wasn't a very good model because he kept moving.

'Give me your finger,' said Sam.

She pressed it into the red paint and then onto the white paper.

It made a red blob.

'Now mine.'

I thought they looked much the same, like two coloured eggs.

'Look closer,' she said.

I bent down to the paper and saw each one had its own pattern of squiggles and circles and lines.

'No two people have the same fingerprint,' said Sam. 'You can never be like someone else.'

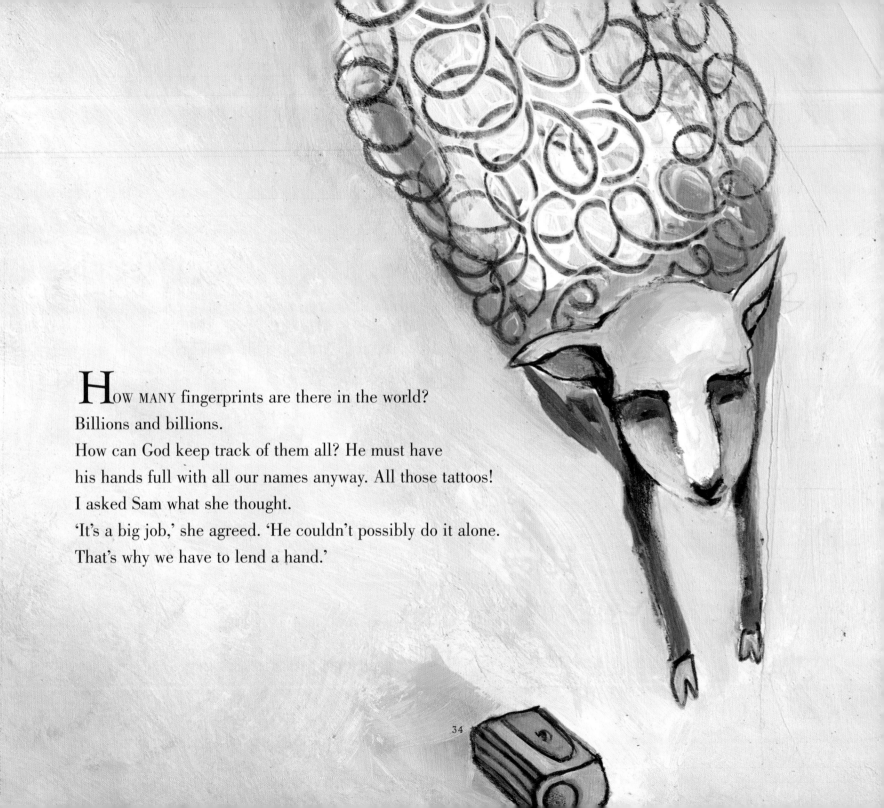

HOW MANY fingerprints are there in the world?
Billions and billions.
How can God keep track of them all? He must have
his hands full with all our names anyway. All those tattoos!
I asked Sam what she thought.
'It's a big job,' she agreed. 'He couldn't possibly do it alone.
That's why we have to lend a hand.'

34

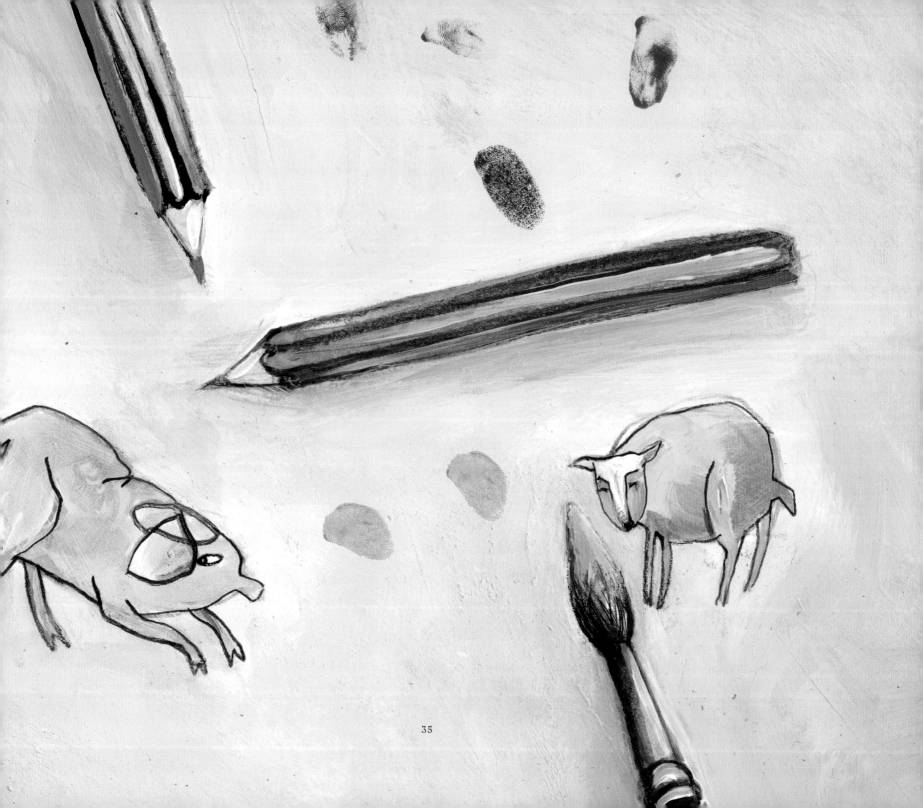

SHE FOUND A PIECE OF PAPER and traced around her hand with a red pen.

Then she traced my hand inside hers.

'See, I'm holding your hand in mine,' she said.

'Where's God's?' I asked.

'It doesn't fit on the paper,' she replied.

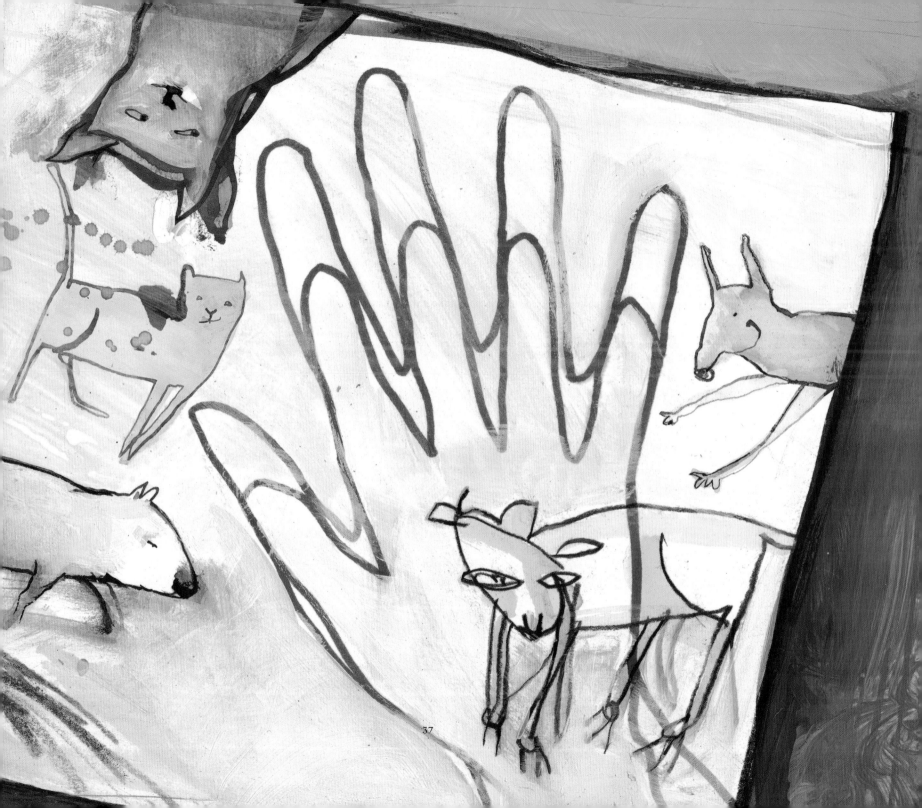

I<small>T'S</small> S<small>AM'S</small> <small>BIRTHDAY NEXT WEEK.</small>

I want to make her the most beautiful card in the world, so I think of the most beautiful thing I know.

I think of those strange black mountains that I can see from her garden. I think of the blue bedroom on the Isle of Skye that I can go to whenever I want. And then I think of our fingerprints.

I got Mum to do hers too. Because she's Sam's best friend. And I got Julie to do hers because she's my best friend. Mum wasn't too keen at first because she was in the middle of a huge pile of ironing and didn't want to get her hands all messy. But she agreed in the end.

The result didn't look too good. It was a bit blotchy. But then I don't suppose God with all his tattoos looks that beautiful either. You've just got to get a bit closer, that's all.

I SENT IT OFF TODAY. A card full of fingerprints. To my godmother Sam.

Text: © S.R.Harris
Illustrations: © Helen van Vliet

Published by S&F
Landsroemlaan 24, 1083 Brussels

First published in 2003

Published in Belgium by NV Uitgeverij Altiora Averbode, postbus 54, 3271 Averbode

British Library Cataloguing in Publication Data
A catalogue record for this book is available from the British Library.

ISBN 90-76875-02-2